Stinky Smelly Feet

A LOVE STORY

BY
Margie Palatini

ILLUSTRATED BY
Ethan Long

DUTTON CHILDREN'S BOOKS

NEW YORK

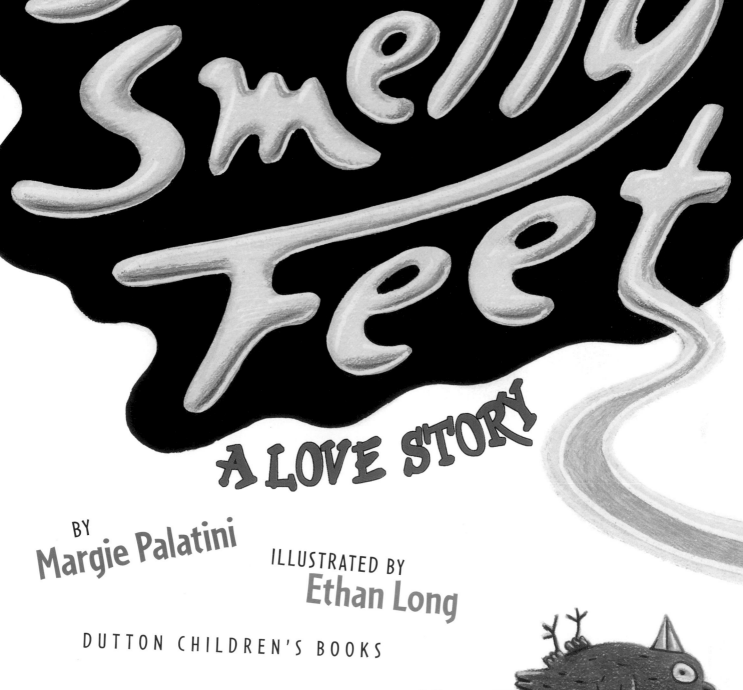

Library of Congress Cataloging-in-Publication Data

Palatini, Margie.
Stinky, smelly feet: a love story/by Margie Palatini; illustrated by Ethan Long.–1st ed.
p. cm.
Summary: When stinky feet threaten the romance between Douglas and Dolores,
they must find a solution.
ISBN 0-525-47201-0
[1. Smell–Fiction. 2. Foot–Fiction. 3. Shoes–Fiction. 4. Humorous stories.] I. Long, Ethan, ill. II. Title.
PZ7.P1755St 2004
[E]–dc22 2003019224

Published in the United States by Dutton Children's Books,
a division of Penguin Young Readers Group
345 Hudson Street, New York, New York 10014
www.penguin.com
Designed by Richard Amari

Manufactured in China
First Edition
1 3 5 7 9 10 8 6 4 2

For my (sometimes) "stinky, smelly"—but "sweetie" of a son

M.P.

For Heather, with love

E.L.

Douglas and his dear friend Dolores
were having a splendid day in the park.

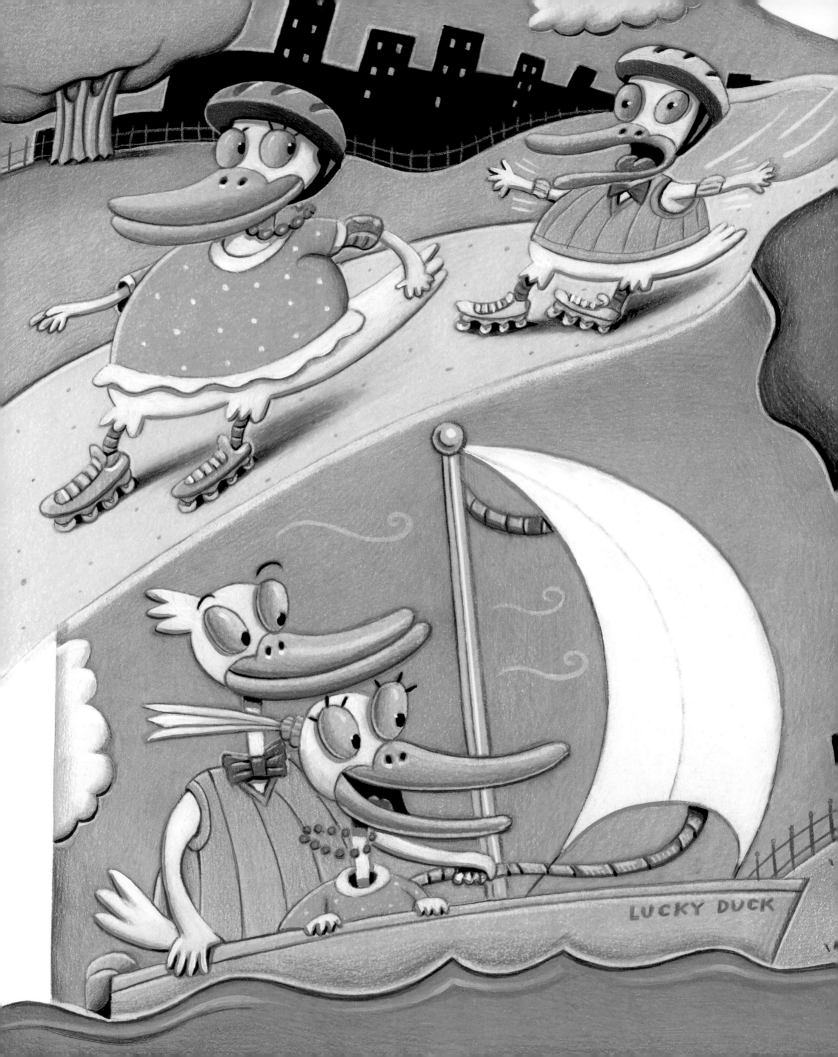

They skated.

They sailed.

They snacked on cucumber-and-butter sandwiches beneath a big, shady tree.

Douglas was quite smitten with Dolores. And one could see that Dolores was quite smitten with Douglas as well.

Dolores giggled. "Let's kick off our shoes and let the grass tickle our toes."

"What fun!" said Douglas. "Yes, let's."

Douglas pulled off his left shoe. He had just flung off his right shoe with carefree abandon when suddenly—

PLUNK!

Down went Dolores.

"Oh my. Oh me," cried Douglas. He fanned Dolores with a napkin to give her some air. "What's wrong, my dear? What's wrong?"

Dolores opened her eyes and mumbled softly.

"Oh my. Oh me. I can't hear you," said Douglas, furiously fanning and waving and waving and fanning.

Dolores mumbled again.

"I still can't hear you," said Douglas with another fan and wave.

Dolores mumbled some more.

"Oh, Dolores, dear, what can I do? What can I do?" cried poor Douglas.

Dolores sat up. She took a deep breath.
"PUT ON YOUR SHOES!" she shouted.
"YOU HAVE STINKY, SMELLY FEET!"

KERPLUNK!

Down again went Dolores.

"Oh my. Oh me," said Douglas. He didn't know what to do first—fan Dolores or put on his shoes.

"Shoes. Shoes," muttered Dolores oh-so-softly.

Shoes it was.

And in no time, Dolores came to.

"That was a close one," she sighed.

Douglas helped Dolores off the ground. She picked a squished cucumber-and-butter sandwich from her hair.

He, of course, was very embarrassed about having stinky, smelly feet.

"Think nothing of it," said Dolores, patting his hand. "But...I do think a bath might be in order."

Douglas was in total agreement. A long, hot, soapy bubble bath, with plenty of bubbles, was surely the cure for those stinky, smelly feet.

After saying adieu to Dolores, Douglas hurried home. He filled the tub and soaked in the hot, soapy water for one whole hour and fifteen minutes.

His feet now smelled quite delightful. Not a bit of stink to be sniffed.

Douglas telephoned Dolores to tell her the good news.

She was very happy to hear it.

"Would you care to take a whiff this evening?" he asked with great confidence.

Dolores ever so politely declined, but she did accept Douglas's invitation to see a movie.

At the theater he bought her a big tub of popcorn, a box of chocolate candies with sprinkles, and a giant soda with two straws.

Yes, it was plain to see that Douglas was smitten with Dolores, and Dolores was indeed very smitten with Douglas as well.

The two sat very close together in row thirteen, which was their favorite number. The theater darkened. The music swelled. The movie was just about to begin when Douglas felt something very uncomfortable under his left big toe.

"Oh my. Oh me," whispered Douglas to Dolores. "I think I have a pebble in my shoe."

"Oh, please do remove it before the movie starts," Dolores whispered back. "That can be so unpleasant."

Douglas untied the laces and slipped his foot out from the shoe. Then suddenly he heard a...

PLOP!

"Oh my. Oh me," gasped Douglas. Dolores was face-first in the popcorn.

PLOP. PLOP. PLOP. PLOP went everyone else in the row alongside Douglas. And the next row. And the next. The next. Next. Next.

There was a loud "PEE-YEW!" followed by a mad rush for the exits.

A policeman in the lobby shouted through a bullhorn,

"YOU IN THERE WITH THOSE STINKY, SMELLY FEET.
COME OUT WITH YOUR SHOES ON!"

Douglas was extremely embarrassed about having stinky, smelly feet. Again. Especially in public.

Dolores pulled a piece of popcorn from her ear and patted his hand. "Perhaps what you need is a bit more powder, my love."

Douglas looked at Dolores. "Perhaps."

So Douglas went home and showered. And powdered. And perfumed. Then sprayed. Sprayed. Sprayed.

His toes were decidedly most fragrant. The most fragrant they had ever been.

He went to sleep that night very happy and pleased, knowing he no longer had stinky, smelly feet.

The very next morning, Douglas knocked on Dolores's door.

"Care to join me for a day at the beach?" he asked with a big grin and sweet feet.

"I would love to," replied Dolores.

So the two packed up their blanket, towels, buckets, and a big striped umbrella, and off they went.

Douglas stuck the umbrella deep into the sand, and he and
Dolores sat under its shade, staring at the ocean and watching
the waves.

They gathered shells.

They built a sand castle for two.

They shared a hot dog with lots of mustard.

Yes, Douglas was very smitten with Dolores. And Dolores was indeed quite smitten with Douglas as well.

She looked into his eyes and said, "Shall we wiggle our toes in the sand?"

Just to be safe, Douglas checked which way the wind was blowing.

Just to be prepared, he handed Dolores a clothespin for her nose.

Alas, it was not enough. When Douglas removed his shoes,
Dolores went down for the third time.
"PEEEEEE-YEWWWW!" cried the crowd.
The lifeguard blew his whistle.

"ABANDON THE BEACH!"

"Water. Water," mumbled a faint Dolores through her clothespinned nostrils.

Douglas grabbed his bucket, hurried to the water's edge, and ran back to Dolores.

SPLASH!

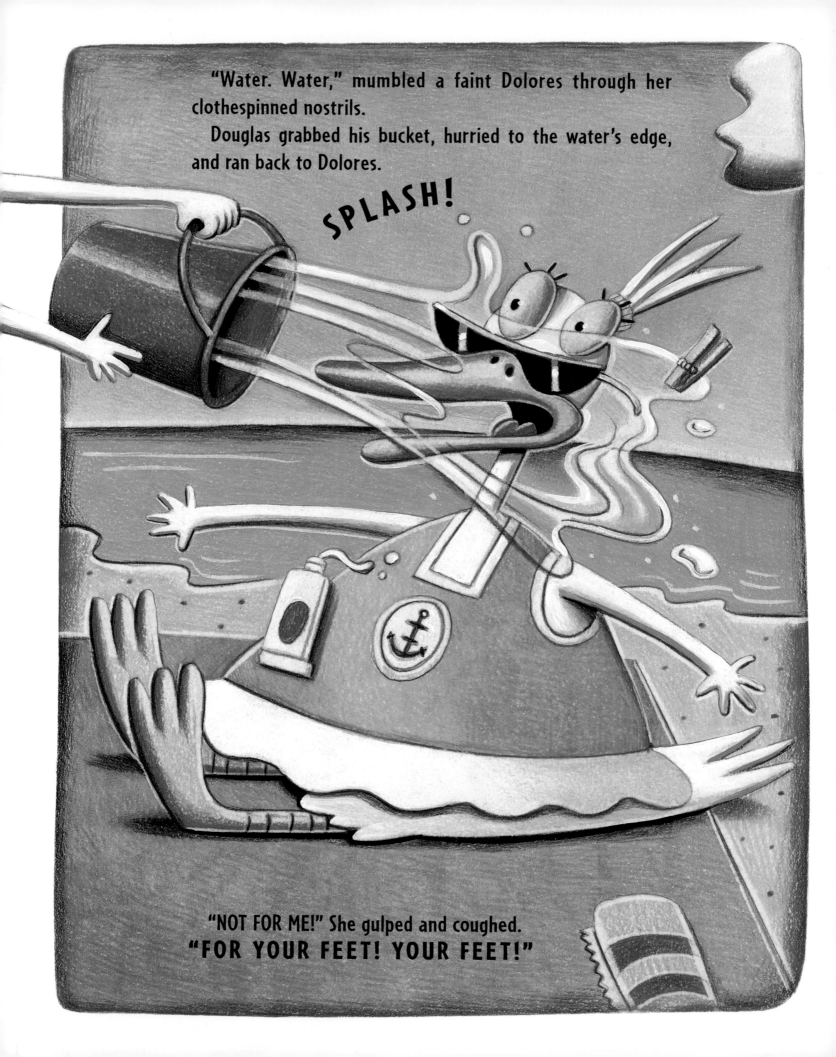

"NOT FOR ME!" She gulped and coughed.
"FOR YOUR FEET! YOUR FEET!"

"Oh my. Oh me," said Douglas, wading sadly into the ocean.
It was not a good day at the beach.
It was not a good day for Douglas and Dolores.

"I have stinky, smelly feet, and that's all there is to it," sighed Douglas after another long, hot, soapy bath.

Dolores sat down next to Douglas, patted his hand, and sighed as well.

They were both quiet. They were both quiet for a long time.

And then Dolores smelled something very bad, very foul, and very nasty.

And it was not Douglas!

It was coming from the bedroom closet. "Aha!" Dolores happily exclaimed as she made the discovery. "I don't think you have stinky, smelly feet at all!"

"Oh my. Oh me. I don't?" said Douglas, very surprised.

Dolores held her nose and shook her head. "No. Not in the least. Your feet are fine. It's your shoes. I believe you have stinky, smelly shoes."

They both sniffed.

They came to and concluded…Yes. It was most definitely the shoes.

So they got rid of the shoes.

Every last stinky pair.

Douglas was more than ever very smitten with Dolores. And Dolores remained very smitten with Douglas as well.

Which was very nice indeed.

Because, as it turned out, Douglas's shoes weren't really the problem.

No.
He still had stinky, smelly feet.
But it did not matter.
For what Douglas and Dolores had was really true love.